KINDERDIKE

LEONARD EVERETT FISHER

Macmillan Publishing Company   New York   Maxwell Macmillan Canada   Toronto

Maxwell Macmillan International   New York   Oxford   Singapore   Sydney

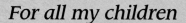

For all my children

Library of Congress Cataloging-in-Publication Data. Fisher, Leonard Everett. Kinderdike / Leonard Everett Fisher. — 1st ed.   p.   cm.   Summary: When a baby and a kitten are found safe and dry after a disastrous flood in 1421, the people of a village in southern Holland decide to rebuild.   ISBN 0-02-735365-6   [1. Folklore— Netherlands. 2. Stories in rhyme.]   I. Title.   PZ8.3.F635Ki   1994   398.21—dc20   [E]   93-8140

A tiny Dutch village stood low near the sea,

where a dike held the tide for a people carefree.

Crisscrossed canals drained seawater away,

helped by a windmill that pumped every day.

Here villagers fished in the summer parch.

Here they skated from December to March.

Then a fearful spring gale flooded the shore,

destroying the windmill, the houses, and more.

But a baby and kitten were heard to cry,

left alone on a dike, safe and dry.

It's a sign to rebuild, the villagers agreed.

They built new houses and planted some seed.

Stronger windmills appeared, nineteen in all,

to pump the water beyond the seawall.

The village was named for the foundling tyke,

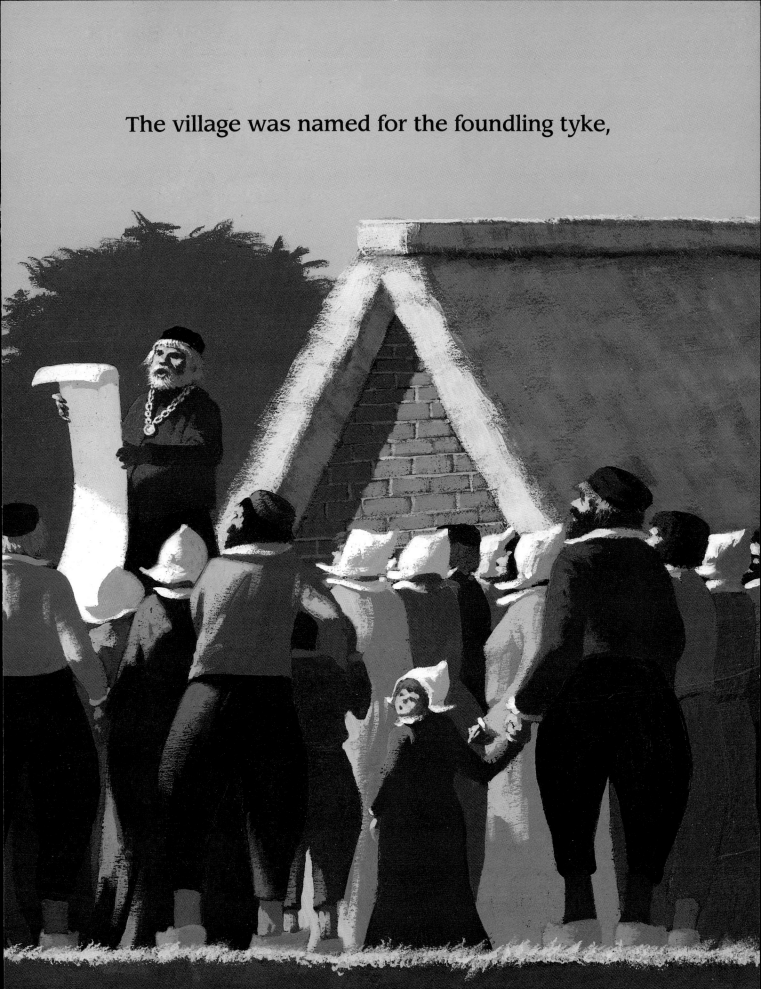

and called forever after, Kinderdike.